Where
the
Durian Tree Grows

Where the the Durian Tree Grows

A Collection of Five Short Stories

Leela Chakrabarty

PARTRIDGE

A Penguin Random House Company

To order additional copies of this book, contact
Toll Free 800 101 2657 (Singapore)
Toll Free 1 800 81 7340 (Malaysia)
orders.singapore@partridgepublishing.com

www.partridgepublishing.com/singapore

Preface

The durian tree is a large tree native to Malaysia that bears the durian fruit. The word *durian* is derived from the word *duri*, which means 'thorn' in the Malay language. This is due to the fact that the fruit has thorns on its outer layer. It is a spiky oval fruit that contains a creamy pulp that is highly valued for its flavour.

This collection of five stories is embedded in a Malaysian setting. The durian fruit is symbolically mentioned in this title, as it is regarded as a symbol of mystique. One should not judge it based on its spiky outer appearance and strange smell that some describe as rancid; the magic begins when you pry open the fruit to reveal a soft, succulent, fleshy yellowish pulp and discover the mystical qualities of what the locals revere as the "King of Fruit".

To my late mother,
Gita Chakrabarty

The Mysterious Farm

Chapter 1

Amir who has just turned sixteen lives with his family in a small village. His family has been involved in a business they inherited from his forefathers. They sell *gula melaka* (palm sugar) that they make by themselves from the sap of the coconut tree. The tapping is done through an incision made on the young coconut shoot. Amir's dad has a worker who climbs up the tall coconut trees to get this done. Then he ties a cylindrical container to the shoot to collect the colourless sap that flows out of the incision.

During processing, heat from the fire is controlled to prevent the sap from getting burnt. The sap turns thick and dark brown in colour after five to six hours.

During school breaks, Amir usually helps with the family business. This morning is just like any other morning. He scoops the molten palm sugar, pours it into small bamboo moulds, and leaves them to cool. The liquid is allowed to thicken until it hardens. The liquefied sugar usually cools down in five minutes. When it hardens, Amir overturns the moulds to take the solidified sugary substance out. This solid mass is dark brown and tastes extremely sweet. This *gula melaka* tastes similar to the brown, solid, sugary substance made from the date palm in the Middle East.

Gula Melaka is largely used in *Peranakan* (Chinese-Malay) cuisine. A popular desert is the *sago gula Melaka* (chilled sago with palm sugar syrup).

Amir then packs the cylindrical solid masses into plastic bags that he then carefully ties up. He places each plastic bag neatly in a cardboard box. Having done so, he carries a few boxes at a time to Mr Yee's provision shop in the village, in which he sells all kinds of household goods and foodstuffs.

Mr Yee greets Amir as Amir walks into his shop. "Hello, Amir. Very early this morning."

"Yes, I guess I am a little early this morning," Amir replies.

"Why are you looking a little down?" Mr Yee asks.

"Well, three of Dad's goats have gone missing. I'm going to help my father look for them," Amir explains.

Many others have complained that their farm animals have gone missing. It is rather puzzling. There is no trace of the animals being attacked.

"Oh, I see!" Mr Yee exclaims.

"Okay then, Mr Yee; see you again." Amir takes the payment that Mr Yee has given him and bids him goodbye.

Chapter 2

Mr. Yee opened his provision shop in this quaint village about fourteen kilometres from the town of Melaka.

Melaka town has a long history and a rich heritage. Here salmon-pink buildings catch the eye. Visitors hear the sizzling of a variety of street food and see people hustling through long shopping streets.

In contrast, this village sits quietly, with traditional houses in between the great, versatile coconut palms.

The coconut tree is a palm with a single, straight trunk. The oil and milk derived from coconuts are commonly used in cooking. All the parts of the tree offer some use. For example, the coconut husk can be used to make scrubbers, ropes, and mats. The thick woody midribs from the leaves can be used to make brooms. There are many other uses.

The next morning, as Amir is stirring the sugary liquid over the heat, he sees a truck pass by. It is a little bit longer than a van or pickup, but the bed is boxed and taller than the cab.

Called a box truck, it is usually used to carry goods. To Amir's surprise, droplets of liquid are dripping from the enclosed truck. He notices that the droplets are a maroon shade of red.

Oh my, he thinks. *Blood red! Could it be what I'm thinking?*

He asks his sister to take over for him and dashes towards his bicycle, which is parked at the back of the house. He tries to see where the truck is going.

Amir and his friends used to play bicycle games in the backyard after school each day, games of their own invention. As a young boy, he learned that it takes the movement of legs to propel the bike forward, and he became good at it. It took many trials and errors and crashes before he mastered the art of bicycling.

At this moment, Amir feels as brave as a knight fighting a dragon. At the same time, he also feels as safe as a soldier in the army, as he is so used to cycling.

But alas, the truck has disappeared into a nearby forested area. Amir is unable to see more. Nevertheless, he is adamant to find out more about the truck and its contents.

The day is oppressively humid, but Amir does not show any sign of giving up. He grew up at the end of this dirt road, so his early bike-riding days were all done on the tricky, bumpy gravel that stretched from his house to Mr Yee's shop at the other end.

"Aha! Here you are."

Amir sees the box truck parked near a shed. A man is unloading some boxes into the shed.

Amir rides his bike towards the shed and stops beside the truck. He confronts the truck driver, who is still seated on the driver's seat, about the blood stain.

The driver tries to avoid answering the question and reprimands Amir rudely. "Hey, who do you think you are?"

"I was just concerned about the blood dripping," Amir tries to explain.

"Well, there's nothing here for you to see. Quick, get lost!" the driver shouts.

"But – " Amir goes on.

Then the truck driver, with cruel, glaring eyes and a menacing expression, begins to threaten him. "Are you crazy? If you don't go now, I'll call the police."

"But I didn't do anything wrong."

"Trying to be clever, eh? I'll say that you tried to steal my goods," the truck driver threatens.

Amir has no choice but to go away. He is very upset by the encounter. All night long, he tosses and turns in his bed, quite sure something is amiss.

Chapter 3

The next morning, Amir is at Mr Yee's shop as usual to sell his palm sugar. He has brought three boxes. Sometimes Mr Yee buys from Amir and sells to other shopkeepers.

Mr Yee greets him as usual. "How are you this morning?"

"Oh, I'm fine, thank you," Amir answers.

Mr Yee turns his focus hurriedly towards the back door as he hears someone call for him. Amir peeks through the aisle of the shop and is startled to see the truck driver from the incident the day before. The truck driver has a brief chat with Mr Yee and disappears quickly.

When Mr Yee returns to the counter, he notices a terrified Amir. "What's wrong, Amir?"

In a distressed voice, Amir replies, "I saw him yesterday."

"Where? Where did you see him?" Mr Yee asks.

"At the shed."

"The shed?" Mr Yee says. "It's far away from here!"

"Oh, you know about the shed?"

"Just tell me what you saw," Mr Yee says.

Amir thinks Mr Yee looks intimidated. "Nothing … I did not see anything. The truck driver was very rude. He did not allow me to see anything. He told me to go away."

"Oh!" Mr Yee looks relieved. "Next time you shouldn't go that far into the jungle. It could be dangerous."

Amir feels there is something unusual about Mr Yee's behaviour. He has a very uneasy feeling, so he decides to investigate further. He takes his bicycle and hits the road, right to the jungle path.

He rides until he is near the shed and then parks his bike a short distance from it. Then he approaches it on foot.

Amir is feeling a little nervous, as Mr Yee warned him that it could be dangerous. Still, he puts forward a brave front and trudges towards the shed.

Just before he gets there, he spots a man walking away from the shed, carrying something that looks like a container. Amir follows the man as carefully and as quietly as he can so he will not be caught.

Chapter 4

The man walks on the jungle trail. The jungle is getting dense, and Amir is worried and nervous. He is afraid that the man he is stalking might notice him.

The trail leads to a big pond. The man stops and stands near the pond. He opens the container, takes out some pieces of meat, and throws them into the pond.

Amir is taken aback when he sees what is in the pond. Large crocodiles are devouring the pieces of meat thrown at them in the pond. The man stands there, feeding the hungry, wild creatures until the container is empty.

Does anyone know about this place? Amir wonders silently.

Amir does not dare stay here any longer. He slowly follows the jungle trail and returns home.

He tells his family about what he saw, but alas, no one believes him. They laugh at him, thinking he is playing a prank.

"I'm telling the truth. I saw it with my own two eyes." Amir tries his best to make them believe him.

"Okay, then—I'll follow you to the crocodile farm," Amir's father says, "and make sure it's there."

The father and son team start their journey into the jungle. Amir's dad reaches for his motorbike, and Amir is the pillion rider. Luckily, Amir remembers the path.

"Let's check out the shed," Amir's dad suggests, sounding like a detective at work.

"Okay, let's go!" Amir replies.

As they reach the shed, they peep into the window, which has been left slightly ajar.

"Oh, there's a large refrigerator in here," Amir's father points out.

"But it doesn't look like the one we use at home," Amir says.

"Yes, this type of freezer is actually used to keep large amounts of meat," his father explains. "They must keep the meat to feed the crocodiles in here."

He gives Amir a solemn look. "I think we should report this matter to the police. Don't know if these people have a licence to keep crocodiles in here." He looks around. "Let's get out of this place quickly."

"Yes, yes!" Amir agrees. "Let's go!"

The duo immediately goes to the police station to report the matter.

The police officer in charge of the case reminds Amir not to tell anyone about what he has seen thus far. Over the next few days, the police department conduct a stakeout, carefully watching the area for suspicious activity.

The police manage to nab the truck driver, and after much questioning, he confesses. He reveals that the crocodiles were actually stolen for Mr Yee from the Melaka Crocodile Farm, more commonly known as *Taman Buaya Melaka*, in Ayer Keroh, a suburb of Melaka. The farm is a home to over a hundred species of crocodiles.

Crocodiles from the farm have been reported missing. The truck driver is one of the accomplices who works at the farm. He has conspired with the unscrupulous Mr. Yee to make some quick cash. They have gotten a few illegal immigrant workers to help them. To cut costs, he had his workers steal farm animals from the villages to feed the crocodiles.

The villagers are very angry when they learn that Mr. Yee has stolen their farm animals merely for his own gain. Mr Yee is a wolf in sheep's clothing. He has not thought about the consequences the villagers have to face or their safety and welfare. Who would have thought the naive-looking Mr. Yee could be a shady criminal?

A Dream Comes True

Chapter 1

There was no sign of wind. The sun was blazing hot. Everything was still. Although Chee Keong's shirt was drenched with sweat, he tirelessly cycled on his rattling old bicycle. Although he was only sixteen, he was a mountain of strength. A huge box was tied up at the back of his bicycle. In the box you could find all kinds of metal objects, mainly empty drink cans.

Chee Keong went house to house pedalling his bicycle to collect these items. Today he had been cycling since two in the afternoon. It was almost four now, but his box was not filled up yet.

Guess luck is not on my side today, he thought.

I must find a little bit more. Otherwise it's really not worth spending so much time and effort.

Just then he saw Madame Salmah in her garden. "Mak Salmah, how are you?"

"I'm fine, how about you? What are you doing cycling in this hot afternoon?"

"I'm collecting empty tin cans. Do you have any, Mak Salmah?" he asked.

"I'm afraid not. I'm sorry."

"What about any metal objects or anything made of steel, perhaps?" Chee Keong did not want to give up.

"Well, let me see!" Madame Salmah said as she looked around. "Ah! Do you want steel pipes? I have some of those in my backyard. I wanted to get rid of them after the renovation. They were left over after I did some renovation to my kitchen," she explained.

"Oh, yes! Please, I definitely want them."

Chee Keong followed Madame Salmah to her backyard. There lay a pile of steel pipes of various sizes as if they had been haphazardly cut; there was also other scrap metal. When Chee Keong saw the pile, he was happy. He picked the pipes up carefully and loaded them into his box. The steel pipes were short ones, so they could fit into the box.

Chee Keong was glad that Madame Salmah had offered him the steel pipes and the other scrap metal. Now he had enough for the day.

"All right, then. See you, Mak Salmah, and thanks a lot!" said Chee Keong.

"I must thank *you*—for clearing up the rubbish," Madame Salmah said jokingly.

"One man's trash is another man's treasure! Rubbish for you, money for me," Chee Keong replied.

"Oh, really? What do you actually do with all these metal objects?" Madame Salmah asked curiously.

"I sell them to a scrap metal recycling factory," Chee Keong explained. "I am paid by the weight of the metal. I get about one ringgit per kilo."

"That's not bad. Don't you go to school?" Madame Salmah asked.

"Yes, I do. I go to school in the morning. Twice a week, I'll go collecting empty cans and metal pieces," Chee Keong explained. "I have to do my schoolwork too at other times, so I'm not able do this every single day. My good friend Rashid follows me on my rounds, but now he is at the mosque to perform his Friday prayers."

"Have you been doing this work for long?"

"No, I've just started. Perhaps, um … about a month ago."

"Do your parents know about this?"

"Well, I don't have a father now. My mum knows. She's not very happy about it, but she does not mind."

"So you are actually helping your mother to supplement the family's income. Is your mother working?"

"She does not go out to work, but she works at home. She sews clothes."

"Oh, a tailor! That's good. Perhaps I can get my clothes to be tailored by her!"

"Of course you can. Please do. If you did, when your clothes were ready, I could bring them over to you. That's what I do to help mum. When the clothes are ready, I deliver them to the customers and collect the payment at the same time," he said with a chuckle.

"Give me your address, then," Madame Salmah asked.

"Oh, yes. We live in that Jalan PK Flats, Block B, flat number 18."

The PK Flats were built to accommodate the lower-income group and squatter folks in the city.

Chapter 2

Madame Salmah, who was in her early forties and dressed in a lovely, printed green *Baju Kurung* (traditional Malay costume), arrived at the doorsteps of Chee Keong's home. She then called out softly, "Hello, is anybody in?"

"Yes, what can I do for you?" a woman replied.

"Oh! Hello. Are you Chee Keong's mother?"

"Yes, I am. And you are …?"

"You can call me Mak Salmah like everyone does. I met Chee Keong the other day, and he told me about the tailoring you do."

"Oh, yes. Chee Keong told me about you. Please come in." Chee Keong's mother invited her in. "I hope you don't mind if I continue with my sewing as we chat."

"Of course not."

Chee Keong's mother was also in her early forties. She had her hair all tied up in a bun, and she looked rather drained that day.

Madame Salmah entered the run-down flats. As she looked around the room, she noticed a young girl painting a picture in the corner.

"Is she your daughter?"

"Yes, she is."

"She is busy painting, I see," Mak Salmah said.

"She is now. She can get quite cranky sometimes. You see, she is a special child," Chee Keong's mum explained. "She needs a lot of attention. That's why I have to stay home to look after her."

"Oh, what kind of problem does she have?"

"She was born with Down syndrome. She has a moderate mental retardation. She is not crazy! But she's slower than the normal children."

"So you have to be very patient with her," Madame Salmah said sympathetically.

"Yes, indeed."

Chee Keong's sister, who was about eleven, was busy painting. Suddenly, she stopped, turned to Madame Salmah, and brought her painting with her. She showed the painting to Madame Salmah.

"Wow! What a pretty drawing. Who is this beautiful lady?"

The little girl pointed at her mother.

"Oh, it's your mother. She must love you so much," Madame Salmah said, looking at Chee Keong's mother.

The little girl nodded, smiling proudly.

"Clever girl!" Madame Salmah said as she patted the girl's shoulder.

Just then Chee Keong returned home from school. His sister ran to him. Chee Keong hugged her as he put his hand in his pocket and took out some sweets. "Here you are – these are for you if you are a good girl!"

His sister took the sweets happily and kissed him on the cheek.

"Oh, hello, Mak Salmah."

"Hello, Chee Keong. I wanted to ask you more about your scrap metal collection. What other kinds of metal objects do you collect?" Mak Salmah asked.

"Steel and tin cans – for example, pet food, baked beans, and sardine cans – they all can be recycled along with aluminium drink cans, empty aerosol cans, and clean aluminium foil plates."

"In that case, why don't you come over to my brother's canteen at Jalan Kebun Secondary School?" Madame Salmah said. "He will definitely have all these type of cans for you."

"Oh, that will be fine!"

"I'll tell him about you. You just go over and collect what you need."

"Okay, Mak Salmah. Thank you very much for your help." Chee Keong said gratefully.

Chapter 3

The next day, Chee Keong cycled to the canteen of the school as Madame Salmah had suggested. He was glad to have done so, as he got quite a lot of empty cans.

Due to hard work, Chee Keong managed to save some money but not enough to start a business. He always wanted to own a shop. Even that little money did not come easy.

He remembered how some boys used to tease him and throw empty cans at him. They had laughed and sneered at him as he cycled on his rounds. They called him all kinds of names, but he pretended not to care. It hurt a lot though. He had to withstand all the hardship, as he wanted to help his mother and look after his sister.

A couple of years had gone by, and Chee Keong had already completed his sixth form, which is equivalent to pre university qualifications, but he was unable to continue his studies due to financial constraints. He did not give up. He kept his fingers crossed.

One day as he was on his rounds, he reached Mr Lim's house. He took some empty tin cans. As he was riding off, he heard some rattling sounds coming from one of the cans. He looked inside it and found an expensive, shiny watch. He knew something was amiss. He saw Maniam working there as the gardener. Maniam used to tease him a lot during his school days.

Was this Maniam's work? Had he purposely hidden the watch here so that he could take it home later, or perhaps he wanted to frame me and make me look like a thief! Chee Keong pondered for a while but did not say a word.

He quietly took it away without letting Maniam notice him. He had never liked Maniam anyway, with his shady character. All the way, he wondered how to return the expensive watch. After much thought he rode down the street to Mr Lim's factory.

Mr Lim was the owner of the scrap metal recycling factory. Mr Lim had known Chee Keong for a long time, as Chee Keong's father used to work in that factory.

As soon as Chee Keong reached the factory, the security guard brought him to the manager's office.

"Sir, this is the thief," the guard said. "Look, he has the watch."

Chee Keong was aghast and on the verge of tears.

"Well, what's your name?" the manager asked.

"Chee Keong, sir."

"When did you steal the watch? You know it's very expensive. Where did you think you could sell it?"

"I did not steal it, sir!"

"Oh, come on. The watch was in your pocket. The watch cannot walk into your pocket, right?" The manager tried to cross-examine him.

Chee Keong tried to defend himself. "No, sir! I did not steal it."

The manager would not listen and contacted the police department immediately. While waiting for the police to come, Chee Keong was taken to a room where he waited. At that moment, Mr Lim walked in into the room, and Maniam was with him.

Immediately Maniam pointed at Chee Keong. "That's the thief," he said.

"How do you know, Maniam?" Mr Lim asked.

"Er … er …." Maniam could not answer.

"I didn't even tell you that there was a theft." Mr Lim began to unfold the puzzle.

The wheels of justice turned slowly.

Mr Lim knew that Maniam had to be the culprit. After much interrogation by the police, Maniam finally spilled the beans. He admitted that two other boys were also involved. They had actually been very jealous of Chee Keong since school days. They used to tease him a lot when they were younger, but he had never reacted.

Mr Lim then offered Chee Keong a job in the factory because he was an honest boy. Although he had found the watch, he did not keep it; he had tried to return it.

Chee Keong worked very hard and got promoted fast. Meanwhile, he continued to study as a part-time student. He got a tiny corner for his sister at Central Market Annexe, Kuala Lumpur. It is a place where visitors can have their portrait done or get their own unique caricature. In Malaysia, Central Market is known as the epicentre of Malaysian culture, arts and handicrafts. It is a popularly known as a must visit destination on every tourist's itinerary. Thus, it is not a surprise that her business began to bloom.

Chee Keong never gave up on wanting to achieve his goals. He had always hoped that someday he would get to own a factory. His dreams came true when Mr Lim grew old and sold off the recycling factory to him.

Chee Keong managed to secure a bank loan to buy the property. He also had some money of his own to supplement the loan. Although it was a small factory, Chee Keong was content and blissful.

An Incident at Mengkabung River

Chapter 1

Aiman and Jeevan are classmates. They are visiting a fishing village near Kota Kinabalu, Sabah, their first experience in East Malaysia.

Kota Kinabalu is the capital of Sabah. It is the commercial and administrative centre of the region. It has industries such as manufacturing furniture, rubber, and plastics. Tourism plays an important role, and there is an international airport. Here is where their plane landed.

As they travelled north from Kota Kinabalu to another town called Tuaran, they saw a few pottery factories. There were many tourists too.

Near Tuaran lies a famous water village. It is called the Mengkabung Water Village. It is a "Bajau" village. From Tuaran it took them a thirty-minute car ride to reach Mengkabung – a "Sea-Bajau" settlement. These people were once sea gypsies who lived on boats or flimsy huts over the shallows. They are the descendant of pirates who set foot here in early nineteenth century.

The water village is a settlement built on stilts bored into the seabed. It has rows of longhouses linked by plank walkways. Transport around the village is by small boats called "sampans." Thus, often the walkways have boats anchored on the sides.

The Mengkabung River has a wide estuary rich with mangrove trees. Here is where the villagers spend their time catching crabs.

As Jeevan and Aiman reached the village, they were introduced to the village headman, En Ako. Jeevan and Aiman were to stay in En Ako's house for two weeks. They were both exhilarated to be in an unusual place. The houses were actually on water!

Jeevan asked, "Are you sure these planks are strong?"

"Of course, they are!" Aiman replied. "People here have been using them for years."

Jeevan, however, was not convinced as he looked at the condition of the planks. "But they look very flimsy."

"Don't worry, it will be okay," Aiman said, trying to make Jeevan feel more comfortable.

"We are surrounded by water!" Jeevan exclaimed, feeling rather awkward.

"Yes, we are. That's the reason why this village is called a 'water' village. All the houses are built on stilts, and these stilts are in the water!" Aiman reiterated.

"I have never seen such a place." Jeevan continued.

"Well, that is one of the reasons we are actually here – to experience something different," Aiman replied matter-of-factly.

Chapter 2

The Mengkabung River is quite a wide river. Mr Ako's son, Madi, was already at the swamps trying to get hold of the crabs. Mr Ako accompanied Aiman and Jeevan to the mangrove swamp.

"Here you are," said Mr Ako. "Look at Madi ... he is already busy!"

"Can we join in?" Aiman asked.

"Of course ... but you must be careful. Don't let the crab pinch you," Mr Ako replied jokingly. The boys were very excited. They watched Madi at first to see how to go about it. Then slowly they tried to catch the crabs on their own.

They were not very good at it. Many times, they slipped and fell into the mud. Nevertheless, they seemed to be having fun.

In the end, they did not manage to catch any crabs. Madi came over to their side and gave them some tips. Actually, the boys were rather afraid of the crabs themselves.

After a while, they gave up and strolled down the river. All of a sudden, Jeevan shouted. "Look, look!"

"What? Where?" Aiman asked in alarm.

"There, over there!" Jeevan said, pointing at the car.

Jeevan was frightened. "Oh, dear! What's going on there?"

"The car is going under—into the water!"

The boys ran hurriedly towards the car, which was slowly sinking.

"Look, Aiman. Look, there's a man walking away."

"Yes, I see that. Why is he walking away from the sinking car? I don't understand."

"Let's see if there's anyone in the car," Jeevan said.

True enough, there was a woman in the car. They called Madi to come to the scene. Madi was a good swimmer. The boys collected some hard solid rocks and passed them to Madi. Madi was indeed a good swimmer. In a few minutes he reached the car, which was already half immersed in the water. He hit the windscreen with a rock and shattered it.

Aiman swam towards Madi and helped Madi pull the woman out of the car. She was unconscious.

Jeevan was not a very good swimmer, so he waited by the riverbank. As soon as Aiman and Madi came to the shore, Jeevan helped them bring the woman up to the land.

Aiman was panting after his exertions. He sat down by the riverbank. "What shall we do now?" he asked.

"I–I don't know," Jeevan replied, "but I think we should inform Mr Ako." He then ran to the house and told Mr Ako while Aiman and Madi waited by the riverbank.

Mr Ako called a boatman to bring the victim to Tuaran, the nearest town. The victim was later taken to a hospital in Kota Kinabalu. The boys then returned to Mr Ako's home.

They told the other villagers how they first saw the car. Aiman was exhausted and wanted to go to bed early. Jeevan, however, was very restless. He was unable to sleep.

"Aiman, was it an accident?" Jeevan asked.

"I don't really know," Aiman replied sleepily.

"Can you remember the man?"

"Yeah …," Aiman replied, his voice barely audible.

"Who was he?"

Aiman did not answer. He was fast asleep.

Chapter 3

The boys – Aiman, Jeevan and Madi – were all required to come to the police station to give their statements, as Mr Ako had contacted the police the day before. The police headquarters was located at Kota Kinabalu.

At the police station, the boys related what had happened.

"About that day, is there anything else that you remember?" the police officer asked.

"Oh, yes." Aiman replied quickly.

"What is it?"

"Well, we saw a man."

"What about the man?"

"He was walking away from the car."

"Will you be able to recognise him if you see him?"

"Perhaps we'll be able to," Aiman answered. "We didn't get very close to him. But I saw his face."

"That's good. Can you describe him?" the police officer asked as another officer brought a sketchpad and sat down in front of the boys. Then he began to sketch the portrait of the man as Aiman and Jeevan described.

"Like this?" the officer asked.

"Yes, almost like that, but his face was a little bit slimmer," Jeevan said.

The officer sketched it again and asked the boys to look at it again.

"Yes!" both of them answered in unison.

When they had finished giving their statements to the police, they asked if they could visit the lady in the hospital. The police officer allowed them to visit her but warned them not to disturb her, as she was still in a coma.

The three boys were escorted by Mr Ako. They visited the victim and were very sad to see her. She was just lying on the bed with lots of gadgets fixed on her body. She was breathing through a respirator.

Mr Ako had something to do in Kota Kinabalu, so he told the boys to go sightseeing for a while and meet up with him later. The boys then stopped by a cafeteria.

As they were eating sandwiches and drinking coffee, they asked Madi a lot about Kota Kinabalu. Suddenly, Jeevan stopped talking, and his face grew pale as if he has seen a ghost.

"What happened, Jeevan?" Aiman asked.

Jeevan was silent. He was looking intently across the room. "Look, that man," he finally said.

When the others turned, they saw no one in particular.

"What man?" Aiman asked.

"There, he was just there. But he is gone."

"Jeevan, what man?"

"The man at the riverbank."

"Where?"

"He was sitting there. I don't know how he managed to disappear so fast."

"Are you seeing things? Maybe you're tired. I think you need a rest," Aiman said.

Chapter 4

Jeevan was disappointed that Aiman did not believe him. After having their snack and drink, they took a stroll down the lane towards the town. After a while, Jeevan was excited again.

"Look, look—there he is!" He pointed at the man he had seen earlier.

"Okay, I see him now," Aiman answered. "He is the one. What is he doing here? Let's follow him."

As they followed the man, they realised that he was walking into the hospital. "What shall we do?" Jeevan asked.

"I think we should inform the police about this matter," Aiman said in a serious tone.

"Yes, I agree. We will wait a while for Mr Ako and go with him to the police station." Just minutes later, Mr Ako returned. They rushed to the police station and reported that they had seen the man from the riverbank at the hospital.

The police did not waste any time. They rushed to the hospital. Thanks to the boys, the police managed to track down the man. He was inside the victim's room, trying to unplug the respirator. He wanted to kill her. If the police had not arrived in time, she would have been killed.

The police apprehended him and brought him to the police station. After a long investigation, the police found out that the man was the victim's husband. She was a very wealthy lady, and he wanted to murder her and get all her properties. The police thanked Aiman, Jeevan, and also Madi for their cooperation with the police.

One of the police officers praised the boys. "You boys have done a good job. Thank you very much."

Chapter 5

After spending their time with En Ako's family, it was time for the boys to return to the peninsular. Just before returning, they visited the 'Tamu', a local market where lots of handicrafts are sold.

Later on, they visited the local pottery making factory. There, the boys tried their skills at making pots.

They were rather bad at it, as they did not have enough skill and patience to shape a beautiful pot.

The boys had a memorable visit to Sabah. A few months later, they each received a letter. It looked very important. They opened their letters and found out something unexpected. They had been invited to a special function at Bukit Aman Police Headquarters.

They were treated as important guests. There was a dinner, and the boys were allowed to bring their parents along. It was a wonderful dinner. Then came the highlight of the night. The names of the boys were called, and they were awarded certificates and a plaque to recognize their bravery for saving the victim of the murder case and cooperating with the police department.

They asked about Madi, as Madi deserved to be honoured too.

One of the officers explained that Madi was not forgotten. "Oh, yes. We did not forget him. He is attending another function in Kota Kinabalu."

Their parents were very proud of their sons. Aiman and Jeevan made their school proud. The principal of their school held a special assembly to announce their good work.

The Young Tutor

Chapter 1

Sarimah lives in Tawau, Sabah. There are some large cocoa plantations here. Most of the cocoa farmers are smallholders. Cocoa products in the state are exported as cocoa beans, and some are processed into cocoa butter and cocoa powder before export. Most of these primary processed cocoa products are sent to peninsular Malaysia for further downstream processing into higher value-added products such as chocolate and chocolate based products.

Madame Chan is one such smallholder of a cocoa plantation. Her plantation is now managed by Mr Kek after the demise of her loving husband, Mr Chan. Madame Chan does not know how to read and write, so she depends a lot on Mr Kek, especially when deals have to be made and signed with other cocoa dealers. She merely leaves her thumbprint when she has to put down her signature. She is rather upset that she cannot even put down her own signature.

Many visitors come to Tawau to visit the cocoa estate at Quoin Hill to see the cocoa trees and tour the factory to learn the fascinating story of cocoa. Cocoa is a very important crop – so important that every year a cocoa festival is held, featuring colourful, cultural dances.

Sarimah and her friends take part in these dances when they are free. Sarimah lives near Madame Chan's house. Sarimah lives in a small plain looking house while Madame Chan lives in a big mansion with many rooms. One of the rooms has been transformed to become the office where she keeps her accounts.

When her husband was alive, he used to handle the business. He set up a home-based office and worked very hard to keep the business going. Now Madame Chan is struggling to keep the business going. She finds it very difficult, as she must constantly depend on Mr Kek.

Chapter 2

"Good morning, Ms Chan!" Sarimah greets her from afar.

"Good morning," she replies softly.

"How are you?"

"Well … I'm fine. I guess." Madame Chan sounds as though she has no energy.

Sarimah continues asking as she approaches. "What happened? You don't sound too good."

"Nothing," Madame Chan says sadly.

"There must be something wrong. You look worried."

"Well … you're right. I'm worried about my cocoa plantation."

"Why? What's wrong with the plantation?"

"I actually don't know. Mr Kek says the business is down. He says the production is low. There seems to be a problem with the cocoa plants."

"But the plants look fine. I see many lorries coming in and out loading the cocoa fruits."

"Yes, that's what I'm thinking. The plants are growing well. The workers are working as usual. But I'm not getting much money anymore. You know, my children are studying abroad. I need a lot of money to support their studies. If this goes on, I will be poor in no time." Madame Chan clearly feels very upset.

"Don't you check the accounts?" Sarimah asks.

"No, I'm not good at figures. I'm not good at anything. I'm going to lose everything that my husband has built," Madame Chan says hopelessly.

"Don't say that. We'll find a way to save everything."

"But how?"

"If you want, I can teach you how to read and write."

"You would?" Mrs. Chan sounds excited.

"Yes, why not? At the moment I'm waiting for my SPM results. After that I wish to study accounts. I'll be glad to teach you what I can."

"Oh! That's great. For a long time I have wanted to learn to read, at least."

Chapter 3

The next day, Madame Chan comes over to Sarimah's house. She brings with her some notebooks and stationery. She is very excited.

"Good morning, Sarimah."

"Good morning, Ms. Chan. Wow, you are all geared up to study, eh?" Sarimah says playfully.

"Yes, yes. I hope I am not disturbing you too early in the morning. I'm very sorry if I'm troubling you."

"Of course not. Please don't worry. You're most welcome," Sarimah says politely.

They sit in front at the veranda of the house and begin their work. Sarimah teaches, and Madame Cham studies. They start from the basics, such as reading and expanding her vocabulary in English.

Madame Chan is very happy to have the chance to improve her reading and writing.

As she is busy studying, a few boys pass by and laugh at her.

"A, apple – B, bear – C, chair …." The boys call out the words and spell them loudly.

"Ha, ha. So old to be studying A-B-Cs," one of them teases.

The boys stand by the front of the veranda, pointing at Madame Chan and laughing. They are amused that such an elderly lady is just beginning to study at an elementary level.

Madame Chan feels so ashamed of herself that she collects her books and leaves. She hides in her room for a long time. Sarimah is confused and doesn't know what to do. She lets Madame Chan be alone for a while.

The next day, she visits Madame Chan and tries to persuade her to study.

"Oh, come on, Ms. Chan. You can't let a few young boys kill your spirits just like that!"

"The boys are right. I am too old to study. It will take a long time to learn to read."

"That's not true. If you put your mind to it, you can do it. Nothing is impossible."

"But I'm too old!" Madame Chan says hesitantly.

Sarimah shakes her head. "It's never too late to study."

"But the little kids are laughing at me."

"We'll solve the problem," Sarimah declares. "From now on, I'll come to your house. We will study in your room. We'll close all the doors. No one can come in and see us study. Is that okay?"

Chapter 4

The duo, Sarimah and Madame Chan, meet on a daily basis. Madame Chan does not allow Sarimah to tell anyone, because she is shy.

After about a month, Madame Chan can read a little and is progressing well. But alas, it is time for Sarimah to leave. She has been accepted by a college to study accounts. Mrs. Chan's hopes are dashed, but Sarimah promises to teach her over the weekends.

In no time, Madame Chan can read. She can even write quite a bit. She can spell her name and write out a signature. She is proud of herself. She still cannot understand much about the credit and debit flow in the accounts, but she doesn't give up. She studies continuously without feeling tired or ashamed anymore.

Meanwhile, Sarimah has finished her intermediate level in accountancy but is unable to further her studies due to financial constraints. So she goes to work for Madame Chan as an accounts clerk. This helps

Madame Chan a lot. In fact, to her relief, Madame Chan learns that the cocoa plantation is actually making money. Sarimah helps her with the accounts.

One day, Madame Chan calls Mr Kek. "Mr Kek, how's the cocoa plantation doing?" she asks calmly.

"Oh, sad to say, not good. We are making a loss now. There isn't any profit," he softly replies.

"Is that so? In that case, I have no choice but ask you to resign."

"Resign, but – but why?"

"You just said we are not making any money."

"But –"

"I'm afraid there's no room for buts. I must lose you. Thank you very much," she says and firmly hangs up.

Mr Kek has no choice but to leave. Madame Chan, and Sarimah clap their hands with joy.

"I don't need Mr Kek, the swindler!" Madame Chan says.

Soon, Madame Chan has hired another manager to look after the plantation. She is grateful to Sarimah for saving her plantation and pays for Sarimah's expenses to further her studies.

Later Sarimah works full-time for Madame Chan. A lot of tourists flock into the plantation to learn more about cocoa. Madame Chan's cocoa plantation continues to make lovely chocolate products for everybody.

At the Dragon Fruit Farm

Chapter 1

Daniel lived in a small village, which was situated very far from the town. The village, called Padang Mewah, was located right at the boundary of Kedah and Thailand. There were many orchards in Padang Mewah. The people here earned money by selling fruits and vegetables.

There were many kinds of fruit trees in the orchards. Some of the people concentrated on one or two kinds of fruits such as durians and mangosteens. Some had orchards with guava and mango trees.

During the harvesting season, a lot of workers were needed to pick the fruits.

It was school holidays. Daniel stopped to pluck a huge ripe guava from a tree and munched. As he was munching the guava, he walked towards a small river.

The water was crystal clear and it murmured down the stream. It was a beautiful morning. The sun was slowly rising. The scenery was very peaceful and tranquil.

Adam was sitting by the river on a huge boulder. He picked up pebbles by the water and threw them into the river. It made a trickling sound.

Adam was thinking very hard. He was wondering how to spend the holiday productively.

Daniel walked towards Adam as he spat out the seeds. "Hello, Adam!" he called.

"Hello, Daniel!" Adam answered.

"What are you doing, sitting here all alone? Don't tell me you are trying to catch fish. You need a fishing line if you want to catch some, you know."

"Well, nothing. I am actually bored sitting here," Adam replied.

When Adam saw the seeds, he remembered Mr Lopez, who owned a fruit plantation. He had many dragon fruit trees in the plantation with different kinds of dragon fruits.

The dragon fruit is an exotic cactus fruit. It has a sweet and mild acidic flavour, similar to the watermelon and kiwi. Most dragon fruit plants flower at night and emit a jasmine-like fragrance.

The fruit itself is round, and its exterior ranges from a dark pink to a reddish colour. The interior colour of dragon fruit ranges from white to pink to magenta. The fruits have tiny, edible black seeds which are very similar to those found inside the kiwi fruit. The fruits in Mr Lopez's orchard were ready for harvesting.

"Daniel, what are you doing during this school holiday?" Adam asked.

"I don't know; I am rather bored," Daniel answered.

"I was just thinking – why don't we go and talk to Mr Lopez."

"What for?"

"You know, it is harvesting time. He always pays boys like us to pick the fruit. We can earn some money. We can use the extra money for our expenses when school reopens."

"That's a good idea. When are you going?" Daniel asked.

"Well, I'm free now. Why don't we walk to his house together?"

"All right, let's go!"

The two boys walked to Mr Lopez's house. As they arrived, they called out for him. It was a big wooden house, full of rooms with big windows. There was a big garden in front of the house.

Mrs Lopez loved gardening. She had planted her garden with all kinds of flowers: roses, multi-coloured daisies, lilies, and even orchids. Her garden was looking very beautiful.

Mr Lopez was short and rather plump, with a big round belly. He was a friendly man. Daniel and Adam greeted him politely.

"Hello, boys! What are you two up to?"

They asked him for the job, and Mr Lopez agreed to hire them.

"You will be paid by the number of dragon fruits that you pick," Mr Lopez explained. "You will get ten sen for each dragon fruit that you pick."

Daniel and Adam agreed. Mr Lopez said they should start work at ten o'clock in the morning. They should continue at two o'clock and work for another hour until three o'clock.

They were both very excited. They were looking forward to earning some extra pocket money. The next day they would be given baskets to fill with dragon fruits.

Chapter 2

The next day, Daniel and Adam got up early to prepare for their first day at work. They had their baths and their breakfast. Then they met each other at a shop near a T-junction. One of the roads at the T-junction led to the orchard.

At ten o'clock sharp, they were at the store where Mr Lopez kept his things. Mr Lopez gave them each a basket and a trolley to bring back the collection. Daniel proudly said that he could collect more than Adam.

At first Adam did not bother to respond to him. His thoughts were more on how many dragon fruits he could pick and earn enough money for the day.

But Daniel seemed to harp on it. "You see, I will collect double the amount you can pick. You always work slowly. I bet you will only earn a few ringgit a day."

Adam was annoyed. "Don't be so sure. What made you say that? Do you want to challenge me?"

"I am not afraid. I have never been lazy in my whole life. Name your bet."

"Wow! You are mad."

"If I can pick more than you, you must give me all your earnings. Agreed?" Daniel asked.

"That's not fair."

"Why? Are you afraid that you will lose to me?" Daniel laughed and started teasing him. "Slow coach, slow coach!"

"I'm not slow." Adam said angrily. "Okay, the bet is on. I'll show you who is slower."

Daniel wanted to earn more than Adam. He rushed and picked as many dragon fruits as he could. After a while he felt tired. He rested and fell asleep. He had only two baskets filled.

Meanwhile, Adam was more organized. He only rested after some time. He made sure that he did not fall asleep. He carried a knapsack along with him, holding a bottle of water and some biscuits. He rested, had a drink, and ate some biscuits. He continued right after that. He was slow and steady so he would not get too tired before it was time to go.

He had lunch at home and returned quickly to continue his work.

Soon it was three o'clock. Daniel returned to the store with six full baskets. Adam only had three baskets filled with large dragon fruits. Adam could not understand what was wrong. He asked, "Daniel, how did you pick so many dragon fruits? I saw you sleeping just now. Did you take mine by mistake?"

"Of course not. How dare you accuse me of stealing? I worked hard. I told you I would pick more than you."

Mr Lopez was there waiting. "Well boys, what is happening?"

"Nothing, Mr Lopez," Adam answered politely.

"Look at Daniel—six baskets! Good job, Daniel. What about you? Adam, you are so lazy. You've collected only three baskets full. Okay, never mind. Let me count, ninety dragon fruits only. So Adam, how much are you going to get?"

"Nine ringgit, sir."

"And you, Daniel? Wow! You have two hundred dragon fruits. That will be twenty ringgit. Adam, you must learn from Daniel. Ask him how he managed to collect so many dragon fruits."

"But Mr Lopez, I did collect the dragon fruits."

"What do you mean?"

"I've collected more than this, but I don't know what happened."

"Adam, you must not try to make excuses. You need to work harder."

"But Mr Lopez –"

"It's okay, Adam, see you tomorrow. If you are lazy again, you are not going to work for me anymore. All the dragon fruits will be rotten by the time you pick them."

Adam was not satisfied. He did not understand how the dragon fruits he picked had gone missing.

Daniel held the money in his hands and arranged the notes in the shape of a fan. Then he fanned them in front of Adam's face. "Look, Adam, look! I told you I would get double what you could get," he said proudly.

He was so proud of himself that he had forgotten that Adam was his friend. He was happy to show off.

Daniel was laughing happily. Adam was disappointed and angry, but he could not do anything. He was thinking hard about how it could have happened. He was sure that Daniel had taken the dragon fruits, but he had no proof.

Chapter 3

The next day, they were back to Mr Lopez's house. This time, Adam was careful, but still the dragon fruits that he had picked for the day were missing. Adam was very disappointed. He thought hard for a while before he realized that someone must have stolen the dragon fruits during lunch time, as he'd gone home to eat during that time and there was no one to look after the fruit.

Daniel was very happy. "Hi, Adam. What are you doing? Look at the money I've earned."

Daniel was showing off the money he had in his hands. Adam did not respond to him. He was really infuriated.

"Daniel, tell me the truth. Did you take the dragon fruits I picked? Please tell me the truth. The dragon fruits cannot move by themselves, you know. You'd better tell the truth."

Daniel got angry and began to throw a punch at Adam. He almost hit him. Adam defended himself by blocking his face with his arm. Then Daniel pushed Adam. Adam fell and immediately stood up and tried to hit Daniel.

There was a struggle between them. Just then, another worker came and stopped the fight.

Daniel insisted that he had not taken the dragon fruits and that Adam was jealous of him.

"Daniel, tomorrow, we will know that you stole the dragon fruits. Mr Lopez will know. I am warning you."

"How will anyone know? Who will believe you?" said Daniel.

Adam was determined to prove that someone had actually stolen the dragon fruits that he had picked.

How do I do that? he thought to himself. *Aha! I will not leave the orchard during lunch. Tomorrow I will bring food so that I can sit there and have my lunch.*

The next day, Adam and Daniel picked the dragon fruits as usual. During lunch, Adam did not go home. He sat under a tree and ate his food. He had packed some sardine sandwiches and a bottle of syrup. Now he was happy. He could watch the dragon fruits. No one could steal them now.

Soon, as usual, it was counting time. This time Daniel had far less than Adam. Immediately, Daniel jumped up. He shouted out loud and said, "You stole my dragon fruits. How come you suddenly have more than me? You, you *slow boy*, you stole my dragon fruits!"

"No, I did not. I did not steal your dragon fruits. I was here all the while doing my work," Adam said.

Then the boys began to argue. Mr Lopez quickly interrupted them.

He said, "Enough, boys. I have no proof of anything. I'll pay you as usual; that is according to the number of dragon fruits that you have picked.

"Adam, I hope you did not steal just to prove that Daniel had stolen from you earlier. I do not encourage such things. Do you understand?"

"Yes, Mr Lopez," Daniel answered obediently.

"Now, both of you go home and come back tomorrow as usual. I don't want any of this nonsense again," Mr. Lopez warned them.

"Tomorrow will be the last day we are collecting anyway!" Daniel shouted and left.

Adam was unhappy. He wanted to tell Mr Lopez that he did not steal the dragon fruits. He was a little angry. He did not want to be labelled as a thief.

I have never done anything wrong in my entire life. I have to do something. This is all wrong. Adam was thinking for a long time. He thought hard.

Finally, he had an idea. He went to a shop and bought a black marker pen. He kept the pen carefully so that he would remember to bring it to work.

He went to work the next day as usual. Daniel was there too, but he was a little late.

Mr Lopez was already at the store waiting for the boys. It was the last day of fruit picking. There were not many more dragon fruits left on the trees.

Chapter 4

Daniel started to pick the dragon fruits slowly. He was whistling away. He was happy that he had a lot of money, and he was going to get much more.

At the end of the day when it was counting time, Adam was rather anxious. After Daniel's collection was counted, it was found that his collection was more than Adam's.

Adam quickly said, "Wait a minute, I have something to say. I made sure that I marked each one of the dragon fruits with a black star. I drew a star on all the dragon fruits I picked. Now, take out and count all the dragon fruits with the black star. They are mine."

Mr Lopez ordered Daniel to do just that. Daniel was ashamed. He tried to dent the marked area at first, but he was not successful. So he separated all the dragon fruits with black stars and counted them.

True enough, there were many dragon fruits that did not belong to Daniel. The dragon fruits that Daniel picked did not have black stars.

Daniel did not know what to do. He stood there quietly.

"Look, I have a black marker pen with me. I drew the stars myself as I picked them," Adam said.

Now Mr Lopez knew the truth. He called Adam over. "I'm sorry for my mistake, Adam. I called you a lazy boy. Actually, you were the hardworking one. Daniel, I will count the total amount you should actually get, and you must return the rest to Adam. Adam, I am going to give you twenty ringgit just for being so smart. You were clever enough to plan something like this."

Daniel was ashamed. He had thought he could cheat and win, but he was wrong. In the end, Adam, who was honest and hardworking, received more money. Daniel was not allowed to work at the orchard anymore.